I0788102

By Tracy Blom

Illustrated and designed by
Fx And Color Studio

1
First Female
Olympic Track And Field Gold Medal

Dedication

To the game changers, barrier breakers, and trailblazers: May you always keep running the great race and never accept anything less than your best. To Betty's children Rick and Jaine; grandchildren Brook, Tucker, and Sawyer; and great-grandchildren. To the Women's Sports Museum for showcasing Betty's accomplishments and inspiring future generations.

Betty "Babe" Robinson

Elizabeth R. Schwartz (Robinson) was an American athlete and the first female runner to take home a gold medal in track and field for the United States. She was a self-taught runner who had a passion for life and elevating both herself and those around her. After chasing down a train on her way to school one day, Betty caught the eye of a racing coach who suggested that she race with the men. That same year, Betty qualified for the 1928 Olympics. Though at that time women had to pay their own way to participate, Betty competed and won the 100m dash, setting a new world record at only sixteen years old.

In 1931, Betty was involved in a plane crash and was told that she would never walk again. Not only did she learn to walk again, but she also ran, later competing in the 1936 Olympic Games. She is a true testament to perseverance, breaking barriers, and overcoming odds. Her strength, determination, and story reminds us of the power that resides in our souls and minds. Betty always said that "mind over matter" is what had helped her overcome so many things, and today we showcase her life's accomplishments to remind future generations of the strength that lies within.

There once was a girl who loved to compete.
She was known as "the fastest girl on two feet."

Her story begins on a cold winter's day,
She was heading to school as the train pulled away.
She chased down the train, since it just wouldn't wait.
She refused to miss school, and she couldn't be late.

Her train-chasing trick had caught the eye
Of an old racing coach who was seated nearby.
"Young lady, that was quite special indeed,
I'd like to time you and record your speed."

He timed her once, then timed her again,
And suggested that Betty race with the men.
Racing was something girls just didn't do,
But Betty loved any challenge she could break through.

Just two weeks later, she raced in a heat,
Astounded at the world record she beat.
Soon she was racing in the Olympic Games,
Where women could race and be treated the same.
She became the first woman to take home a gold,
And broke several world records at sixteen years old.

376
879
461
1
2
3

There were parades and parties to honor her name,
But she always stayed kind, treating people the same.

Then, one hot summer day in July,
She went up in a plane and soared through the sky.
They were nearly six hundred feet off of the ground
When the engine went out and they came crashing down!

042

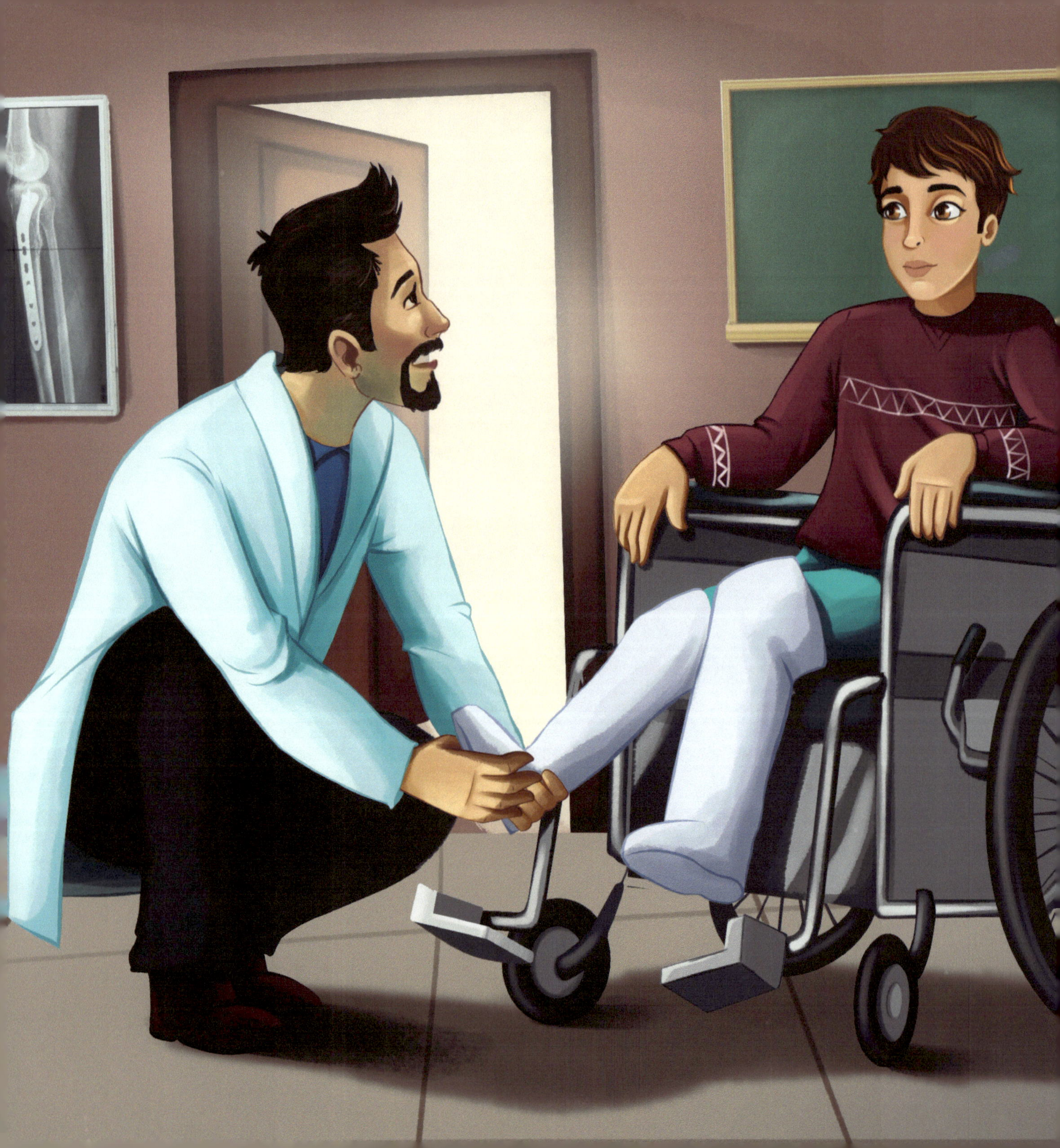

They thought she was dead, but she was alive!
It was nearly impossible that she had survived.
And when she awoke, she was given bad news:
Her legs, they were broken… held together with screws.
"You won't walk again, and you surely won't run,
Not with the damage the plane crash has done."

But Betty was determined to walk once more,
And within six months her feet touched the floor!

She walked, then she ran, with her dad by her side,
And within five years, she was back in full stride.

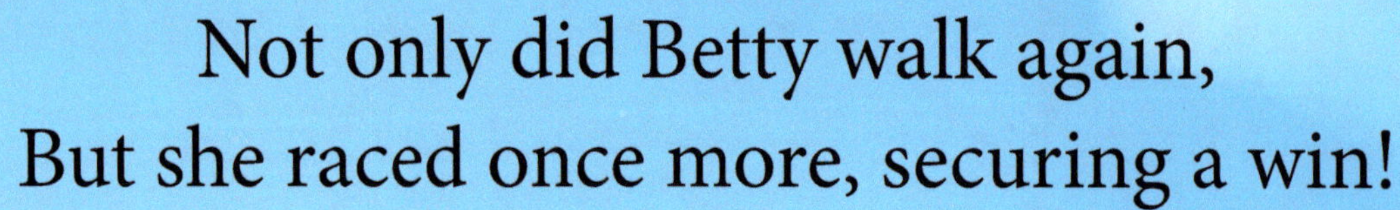

Not only did Betty walk again,
But she raced once more, securing a win!

Betty never was boastful, always humble and kind.
She believed that all power begins in the mind.
She held on to her medals of silver and gold
And tucked them away until she grew old,
Only bringing them out every once in a while
To share with her kids, to make them all smile.

Today we look back on all that she did,
Winning Olympic medals when she was a kid,
Racing with men when they said she shouldn't,
And walking again when they said she couldn't.
Her story reminds us to rise above fears
And will inspire us all for years and years.

www.ingramcontent.com/pod-product-compliance
Lightning Source LLC
Chambersburg PA
CBHW041425300726
48981CB00008B/405